See the Dog

Three Stories About a Cat

David LaRochelle

illustrated by Mike Wohnoutka

CANDLEWICK PRESS

Story Number One

See the Dog

See the dog.

See the dog run.

See the dog bark.

See the dog
dig a hole.

See the dog
dig a hole NOW.

STAND BACK, EVERY-ONE!

Here comes the digging dog!

See the dog
STOP
digging holes!

Story Number Two

See the Lake

See the lake.

See the dog
swim across the lake
to get the stick.

Jump in, dog!

Swim, dog, swim!

See the dog
get the stick.

Story Number Three

See the Sheep

See the sheep.

See the brave dog
protect the sheep.

See the brave dog protect the sheep from the wolf.

Watch out, dog.
The wolf is getting
closer.

The wolf is almost here!

IT'S THE WOLF!

Wait a minute.
It's not the wolf.
It's the real dog.

Welcome back, dog!

See the real dog
protect the sheep.

And see the sick cat
get some rest.

To Gary Nygaard, who is still the best friend of all
DL

For my uncle Jimmy, who was always supportive of my books
and especially liked the funny ones
MW

First edition 2021

Library of Congress Catalog Card Number pending
ISBN 978-1-5362-1629-5

21 22 23 24 25 26 CCP 10 9 8 7 6 5 4 3 2 1

Printed in Shenzhen, Guangdong, China

This book was typeset in Myriad and Coop Forged.
The illustrations were done in gouache.

Candlewick Press
99 Dover Street
Somerville, Massachusetts 02144

www.candlewick.com